DARK SHADOWS

NOCTURNAL SCREAMS VOL 3

Mark Leslie

PUBLISHING

For Laurie Blake, a natural born storyteller whose brilliantly ghostly campfire tales still cause shivers all these decades later.

Table of Contents

Introduction

WHEN I PUBLISHED *One Hand Screaming*, my first book, which is a collection of macabre stories and poems, I confessed that I screamed a lot. I called them silent screams. I said that story ideas bounced around inside my head like an impending storm, brewing into a force that will escape in a wild dance of chaos if I didn't stop to write them down.

It has always seemed to be that way for me when I was writing fiction.

No matter what the story I was trying to write, something in me was drawn towards the shadows.

An author friend of mine, Nancy Kilpatrick, who wrote a nice blurb for *One Hand Screaming* wrote the following: "Mark Leslie's horror is reminiscent of the old-time story tellers, those guys who cared about plot, and were pretty good at building a creepy tale. If there's a dark corner, Leslie will draw you to it, even against your will."

I quite like that last sentence. Because it nicely captures how I, as a writer, I am drawn to the dark corners. That, even against my own will, I find myself moving in that direction, pursuing the shadows.

In this third collection in the *Nocturnal Screams* series, I wanted to share three stories that involve dark shadows. The first two stories involve shadows themselves, and the third involves a different sort of shadow, the shadows caused by a thick and creeping fog at night.

The Shadow Men is a story that I wrote as a spin-off for a longer story I had published years earlier called *Erratic Cycles*. It was drawn from the mythology that is eluded to briefly in that longer piece, and the concept was something I couldn't leave alone, so I had to write it.

In the tale *Follow the Shadow* I wanted to explore the concept of whether or not the shadow follows the person, or the person follows the shadow. It, too, is another relatively short piece and more moody in nature.

The final story, the longest one here, coming in at approximately ten thousand words, is *A Murder of Scarecrows*. This one, the one that takes place in the shadowy fog of a cool dark summer night on the eastern cost of Canada, is a longer piece with a lot more character development.

The full stories-behind-the-stories will appear at the end of this book. That's where I will reveal to you some insights behind the inspiration and what I was attempting to do when crafting the tales.

But those are for *after* you finish the stories, if you so choose to explore deeper and beyond.

For now, take my hand, lets step out into the night and marvel at how, as we walk down the street, the moon and the streetlights take turns making our shadows dance and slither along the pavement beside us in different directions as we walk together. Let's pay attention to the tales, but let's continue to cast curious glances at the beings that creep up from where our feet touch the ground, if only to see where our shadows might move to next.

The Shadow Men

I'LL NEVER FORGET the night that changed my life forever. It happened in the woods when I was ten years old.

It was dark; the air was crisp and chilly. Curious little sounds cut through the night – small animals rustling in the nearby bushes, the haunting call of a loon on the lake, leaves whispering in the breeze. And the air was charged with the smell of the still-burning embers of a recently doused campfire.

It was a night, in fact, not all that different than tonight.

I was sleeping in a four-man tent with my parents and younger brother and woke up with an overwhelming urge to pee. I crawled out of my sleeping bag, careful not to wake anyone else, slipped outside the tent and headed down the moonlit path to where I remembered the outhouse was.

Before I took more than a dozen steps I heard a noise behind me: the crack of a branch breaking underfoot.

With my hairs standing on edge, I managed not to let out a yelp as I turned.

There on the path not three steps behind me stood my little brother, a look on his cute button-nosed face like I'd just caught him sneaking a treat from the cookie jar.

"Jimmy," I whispered. "What are you doing?"

He stood with his right leg partially crossed over the left.

"Need to pee," he said, shifting his weight from foot to foot.

"Geez, Jimmy. If you had to go that bad, why'd you wait so long?"

"Because," he said, his six-year-old eyes wide and bright in the reflected moonlight, "the *Shadow Men* might get me."

I felt a shiver run down my spine despite the fact that I knew the *Shadow Men* were something my father had conjured up that evening around the campfire. They were the bogeyman of the New Hampshire wilderness that hid behind trees and lurked in the shadows. Their sole purpose was to trick little boys down the wrong path in the woods, deeper and deeper into the forest and far from the safety of their parents.

Even at ten, I knew my father told the story to use for fun and perhaps partially to keep us from wandering far away from them; but when Jimmy said that I still felt a chill.

"The *Shadow Men* aren't real, Jimmy."

"Are too! Listen!"

At just that moment the haunting call of a loon echoed through the forest, delivering a deep shiver up the base of my spine.

"That's just a loon," I said, but the chill wouldn't go away.

"No. Listen, Charlie. It's a little boy. One that the *Shadow Men* tricked. He's warning us."

Frustrated with my brother – and, okay, a little frightened – I just wanted it to end; I didn't want to hear any more. So I thought I'd throw a good scare into him.

I turned and ran down the path. "Jimmy!" I called out. "Behind you! The *Shadow Men* are behind you!"

He let out a cry. "Wait!"

Able to see the path clearly in the moonlight, I ran fast, took a sharp turn and ducked down behind a low bush. Jimmy ran past me, still calling ahead on the trail for me to stop, panic rising in his voice as he seemed to think I'd gotten really far ahead of him. I had to put my hands on my mouth to suppress a laugh. But I stayed silent that way, listening to the padding of his footfalls on the packed dirt path and his calls for me to wait for him receding into the darkness.

His last cry was drowned out by the shrill call of a loon in the distance.

And I never saw him again.

But I hear him all the time.

Now, every time I'm out in the wilderness, out camping, I can hear my little brother's voice. Somewhere, masked within the sad, mournful, unearthly half-laughing, half-wailing cry of a loon, I can hear my little brother warning me that the *Shadow Men* are near.

Just listen for it and tell me what *you* hear.

Follow the Shadow

I WATCHED MY shadow kill a man this morning; strangle him, actually.

Let me tell you, it's not something I enjoyed watching. I made sure not to look into the man's eyes as the thumbs pressed deeper and deeper into his throat, cutting off his oxygen.

I focused, instead, on the man's shadow – it's easier to watch their shadows when they're being killed – but his flailing arms kept invading my vision.

When it was over, I looked down at my own hands, covered in his sweat and drool, my thumbs coated in a thin layer of his blood where my nails had penetrated the skin of his neck, and I simply couldn't believe it.

How could my shadow do such a thing?

I bet you don't believe me, but it's true.

You probably think I'm some looney who is not willing to take responsibility for his own actions. I would readily take the blame if I was the one responsible, but I was merely doing what I was forced to do.

Forced to do by my shadow.

Everyone takes it for granted that their shadow is merely something that tags along and mimics, in perfect time, everyone you do. Mine used to be like that. God, how I long for those days when I could walk in the sun and watch my shadow wrinkle itself along either in front of me or behind; when I could rest assured that it would do exactly as I did, in perfect time.

But now, I'm an unwilling slave to my shadow's every whim.

Don't ask me how it controls my actions, because I couldn't tell you. All I can tell you is that one evening I was walking normally down the street, watching my shadow thrown on the path in front of me by a streetlight, when the shadow of my right arm lifted up over my head. This confused me at first. Then I realized that my right arm was moving in response to this shadowy motion, without my ever willing it to do so.

Then the shadow arm came down, and so did my own.

That was about two weeks ago.

Since then, I started paying more attention to my shadow whenever it was evident, and I'd notice little things, like an arm movement this way or a step that way. Each time, my body responded as if I were the shadow. Once, I tried not to respond to my shadow's motion and felt a strong pulling sensation that almost ripped my limbs from my body. And then, just after making the attempt, my shadow hand delivered a sold punch to my shadow face, and my body painfully complied.

My shadow self obviously does not tolerate resistance.

The lesson was clear. Follow the shadow or suffer.

I wondered if the shadow could get into my thoughts, because I'd started to devise a plan. Simply, I intended on getting myself into complete darkness – thus not allowing myself to have a shadow at all. The shadow must not have been able to read more than concentrated conscious efforts of physical movement on my part, because I was able to confine myself to a basement room in my house without any windows and with the lights off.

And it worked.

Until this morning.

You see, things came on so suddenly that I hadn't had time to formally institute my plan. It was far from foolproof. Sure, I'd secured myself away in windowless basement room with enough food to last about a week and with a connecting bathroom. But I hadn't counted on the fact that one of my family members would find it strange that I had disappeared and show up looking for me.

I'd been sitting in my room in the dark when I heard a voice calling. "Derek! Derek! Are you in here?"

I was my brother Larry. He must have let himself into my house with the key he knew was hidden under the bottom step of the front porch.

I called out to him. "Go away, Larry."

"Derek. What's wrong? Where have you been for the past few days? You haven't answered any phone calls. We've been worried sick about you." His voice was getting louder, closer to the door. There was no lock on it, so I put my entire weight up against it.

"I'm fine. Please just leave me alone."

He tried the door and it budged slightly, but I was able to keep it closed.

"I'm here to help, Derek. Please let me help you. Let me in."

"Go away! I'm serious. Get the hell out of my house! I'm fine."

The doorknob stopped turning and his weight left the other side of the door. Then, without further warning, the door crashed open. He must have charged at the door. I stumbled backwards, covering my eyes.

"Get out! Now! Get out Larry!"

"I think you've missed taking your meds, Derek. I've got them right here . . ."

But it was too late. Before he could get any more words out, my shadow had moved its way over to him, my body following, and reached out to grab his throat. By the time my eyes adjusted to the light, his own eyes were bulging and his face was purple. I found it easier to look away, focusing on his shadow; but like I said, his flailing arms were inevitably crossing into my line of sight.

He died.

I watched my shadow let go of his shadow and he dropped to the floor.

I had learned my second lesson.

Don't deny the shadow its rightful existence.

Or else.

I'm writing this message and emailing it to everyone in my address book, posting it on as many newsgroups as I can, because I have no idea what my shadow will have me do next, or how much longer I can have partial control of my own actions. I only know that I'm slave to my shadow's every whim, and that these whims come at random.

While I can still do this, I wanted some record of my innocence in case I am unable to defend myself later.

And to leave you with a warning.

Be careful on whose shadow you next step.

A Murder of Scarecrows

WHEN WILSON KENDRICK woke to the subtle yet distinct thump in the middle of the night he threw aside the sheets and pattered across the chilled hardwood floor toward the window. He expected to see the Saundersons arriving home late from one of their semi-regular family trips to Maine; or perhaps the driver of a car stalled on the stretch of Highway 7 adjacent to his property.

What he saw in the pale moonlight, instead, were a dozen people scattered about the vast lawn, completely still and unmoving.

Squinting to make out details through the foggy darkness, he changed his mind.

It wasn't a group of people, it was a group of scarecrows.

No, not a group. The term commonly used for a group of crows came to mind.

It was a murder of scarecrows.

A shudder crawled up the base of his spine and cumulated in the reflexive shirking of his shoulder blades.

He stood at the window, not sure what he was going to do; uncertain what a person should do in such a circumstance.

He bided his time by squinting through the window and counting the still, silent sentinels in his yard.

There were thirteen of them.

Deciding he wasn't going to be able to get back to sleep, he took off his pajamas and pulled on the pair of jeans and the neatly pressed t-shirt laid out on the trunk at the end of his bed.

Fully dressed, he walked back to the window to do another head count.

"One, two, three . . ." he counted quietly under his breath, his thin boney finger tapping the window pane as he moved it about pinpointing each still figure in the crosshairs of his vision, ". . . thirteen, fourteen, fifteen, sixteen."

Sixteen?

Something was wrong. He could see himself miscounting by one or two perhaps, but not by three.

He turned around and opened his bedside drawer for the pad of paper and a pencil which he kept to jot down his dreams whenever he woke in the middle of the night. Not that he'd used the pencil and notepad in months; a deep, relaxed sleeper, Wilson rarely remembered his dreams – he just felt good knowing it was there in the drawer, just in case.

He returned to the window and did a recount, this time placing a short mark on the page for each scarecrow he counted.

The count this time was eighteen.

"What's going on?"

He let out a short laugh as he realized what must be happening. A group of local kids must be having fun with him, playing a prank on the middle-aged stranger from out of town who'd moved into their neighborhood earlier that year. It was fall now and perhaps a town tradition to spook the new guy in town during October. He must have caught them in the middle of the act.

He wondered if he should change back into his pajamas and crawl into bed; let them have their fun prank and watch his "surprise" in the morning to see an army of scarecrows in his front yard. He wondered if perhaps a whole group of folks from town might be rising early to be there to see his reaction and extend their official welcome.

But he was too curious.

He wanted to see how they were doing it – particularly, how they were doing it so quickly. He thought of those exposés on the crop circles, on how a very small group of people using just a board and a rope could create intricate patterns in a wheat field, completely baffling authorities for years. Perhaps the scarecrow planters used similarly ingenious techniques.

He giggled in anticipation of what he'd learn catching them in the act as he retrieved his jacket from the front hall closet. But before he opened the front door, he changed his mind, thinking it might be better to sneak out the back door. That might give him a bit more cover, a chance to see how they were doing it before they detected him.

Wilson was methodical, analytical and studious like his father, Graham who was a steadfast engineer until the day he'd died. Wilson, of course, had loved his father deeply, and ended up taking computer engineering courses in an attempt to please the old man who'd hardly ever spoken a kind or loving word to his son.

To Graham Kendrick, being a good father hadn't been about providing a loving and nurturing environment, but about ensuring the child was provided with the proper series of stimuli and the appropriate opportunity to manipulate and explore the physical world around him. Instead of cuddles and hugs, Wilson received books and magazines. In place of loving words and encouragement, he received construction toys and computer components.

Wilson would always remember that spring when he was in grade 8 and his classmates were chatting delightedly about their summer spent playing baseball and football and going swimming and hiking and riding their bikes. That was the summer Wilson spent diligently disassembling and reassembling the Commodore Pet computer. Only once he completed that task would his father allow him the opportunity to actually use the computer and discover the programming languages of BASIC, COBOL, FORTRAN and Pascal. At the tail end of the summer, his father's treat to him, upon passing the test, was allowing him to examine the programming code of the various rudimentary games for this system.

"You'll appreciate playing the games when you understand how they work," Graham Kendrick told his son.

"But Father," Wilson moaned. "Can't I just play the game first? Just for a few minutes."

The old man simply shook his head. "Learn the code first. Make detailed notes. Once I read your notes I'll decide if you're ready to play."

The joys and wonders of creating new landscapes and environments via programming eventually captured Wilson's imagination, and despite his initial frustration, he was eventually thankful to his father for pushing him.

Of course, it wasn't until much later in his career as a programmer that Wilson realized his mother's own passion for studying and writing haiku and renga also had a deep influence on him. Renga, a form of Japanese collaborative poetry, was not unlike the discipline required when working on a piece of programming code that was part of a greater piece of software.

Wilson actually derived the name of his software company, Daisan from a renga term referring to the third stanza of a renga which allowed the next collaborative poet greater freedom. And that is exactly how Wilson had earned himself and his two partners a small fortune. Their concept of channeling shareware and open source code programming through an integrated desktop application directly linking programmers with each other to provide instantaneous wiki-like feedback from around the world was viral in its use. This shared real-time collaboration resulted in stronger, quicker generational growth in programs, and provided greater opportunities for developing programmers all over the world to become recognized by large software companies.

The rising success of Daisan led to the sale of the company to a large platform enterprise. This allowed Wilson to retire at forty-five and pursue other passions; researching his family history led him to this small eastern seaboard town in Nova

Scotia, Canada, where his Scottish father had grown up and met his Japanese mother.

Of course, the other passion that led him to Nova Scotia was the beautiful Ashley; the only woman Wilson had ever loved, and who still held a central place in his heart. He'd met Ashley on his first visit to Halifax ten years earlier, and returned in the hope of winning her love. But when he arrived to learn that ship had sailed a long time ago, he focused instead on the family research.

He slowly cracked open the back door and peeked out. There was less fog in the back yard and the moonlight shone down like a flood-light in the sprawling knolls of his property.

He spotted a figure moving near the grey birch tree just a few yards away. But he realized it wasn't one of the pranksters. Instead, it was another scarecrow, its one arm blowing in a gentle breeze.

He scanned the rest of the yard. At least another dozen scarecrows were scattered about; some standing beside trees, others in the middle of the open expanses of fields.

He slipped out the door and shut it quickly.

Standing on the cement of the back-stoop Wilson breathed in the salty sea air; a habit formed quickly on his very first trip to the east coast and something he unconsciously repeated with each initial step outside.

Able to see more of the yard, and more of the figures scattered about, he realized there must be at least two dozen of the sentries standing guard back there.

Wilson again surveyed the yard for any sign of movement and listened for any noise. It was a calm, quiet night, and there was no sound of rustling footsteps in the leaves or any other indication that there were pranksters moving about in the dark. Wilson heard a car moving down the highway that ran past his house, and the distant resonance of the waves on the nearby shoreline, subtly muted by the fog. A temporary shift in the wind brought with it a strange faint clicking noise like a chorus of knitting needles. It brought to mind the image of an arena filled with a thousand grandmotherly ladies, busily knitting away. Then the noise was gone just as quickly and the night was silent.

Damn, they're good. Really good, he thought, unable to detect any movement other than the occasional scarecrow arm moving in the wind.

Confident that none of the pranksters were within eyesight, he crept cautiously to the nearest grey birch. They must have an entire barn full of these scarecrows, Wilson bemused, beginning to note the neighboring farms likely to be able to hold such an army.

When he got closer to the scarecrow near the tree he was startled to see how realistic her design was.

This scarecrow was dressed like a middle-aged woman in a pale blue suit jacket with a pink button down dress shirt. She had brown wavy hair and large white loop earrings. Her face was flesh colored, some sort of latex; she had eyebrows and painted red lips and glassy bead eyes that reflected the moonlight. As he leaned in to study her face, he detected the faint scent of mothballs and thought he saw a subtle movement in her eyes he figured was the effect of a wisp of cloud passing in front of the moon.

He spent a few moments staring at this woman before he turned to see a figure a few feet to the right he hadn't noticed earlier; a man in a blue tartan shirt with a grey checked sport coat. Wilson took a few steps toward him.

The man had a large nose, grey black hair, big brown eyes and also gave off the subtle scent of mothballs. His mouth was partially opened revealing a set of pearly white teeth. How cleverly realistic, Wilson thought, reaching up and touching the man's latex face.

Wilson jerked his hand back.

The scarecrow's face was warm to the touch.

He pressed a finger onto the man's cheek and left it there.

Yes, definitely warm.

He tried to find the line of where the man's mask ended somewhere past his chin, near his neck. But he could spy no line, no edge. The warm latex disappeared beneath the man's shirt collar without a wrinkle.

Just then a cough echoed through the fog, startling Wilson.

One of the pranksters, he figured, turning to walk back to his house when he bumped into someone.

"Oufff," he stepped back to look at the figure, a tall male scarecrow in a beige suit coat and a pressed white dress shirt with billowing black hair and large dark eyes.

It had definitely not been there a moment before.

Wilson quickly panned his head left and then right, looking for any sign of one of the pranksters. "How the hell are you doing this?" he asked.

Despite the scientific and analytic approach his mind harkened back to folklore of the yūrei from his mother's culture and of which she told the best campfire ghost stories. Wilson had enjoyed the creepy tales about the white dressed ghosts with long disheveled hair but had never wasted a moment's thought believing them. He'd studied the different categories of yūrei but did so more out of a desire to understand his maternal heritage than of any particular interest in the fables.

Only the scarecrow in front of him brought to mind the goryō, the vengeful ghosts of the aristocratic class, and he subconsciously took two steps back before bolting for his back door, memories of his mother's ghost stories and the legends he'd read up on finally overcoming reason and logic.

☠   ☠   ☠

"It's the Swamp Soggon!" Dale shouted, his voice loud over the static filled phone line.

Wilson couldn't think of whom to call other than the young man who tended to the landscaping and various other handyman jobs required on the farmstead. Wilson was a quick study but he'd never been one to work with his hands. Circuit boards were one thing, but wooden boards were an entirely different beast. Outside of electronics, Wilson's idea of a full toolbox was a roll of masking tape, a hammer and a flathead screwdriver.

"The what?" Wilson asked.

"Swamp Soggon. It's a local legend started by Angella Geddes. Up until a half dozen years ago she lived just down the highway in Necum Teuch. She told the tale of a selfish swamp creature with plans to turn all the townsfolk into scarecrows."

Wilson just closed his eyes and shook his head.

He'd needed to call someone, and so had contacted Dale. He figured the young man might have some sort of handle on the prankster's style and methodology, that he was likely to know exactly who was involved. But instead the young man was going on all half-cocked about some sort of swamp creature.

Wilson momentarily wondered if perhaps Dale was in on the hoax, a part of the prank. But he shook that thought off easily when he heard the young man continue.

Dale started rambling in a chopped and anxious tone Wilson had heard only once before from the young man. "I'd always thought those stories were a lark, something the old lady cooked up for fun, for enjoyment, to amuse neighbors, to attract tourists. I had no idea the Swamp Soggon was actually real."

As Dale continued to rave about the old woman's mythology in slow repetitive cycles, Wilson thought back to the only other time he'd heard that same panic in the young man's voice.

It had been earlier in the summer, a particularly hot day in mid July and Dale had been doing various maintenance tasks around the yard. At noon, Wilson had gone looking for the young man, bearing lunch and a portable magnetic chess set when he heard, very faintly, Dale's panicked muffled yells.

The calls had come from the root cellar, a five by eight-foot storage space partially dug into a small knoll far back on the property that you could only get into by dropping into a small ditch and crawling under the wall.

As Wilson got closer he could hear a low steady throbbing that at first sounded like an engine.

Wasps. Hundreds of them. Inside the wall of the root cellar.

It took over an hour for Wilson to convince Dale to climb back down under the wall to get out, that the wasps were so busy banging against the sides of the wall that they wouldn't notice him if he was did it quickly enough.

Dale got out without a single sting, but Wilson never forgot the intense panic in the young man's voice that afternoon.

The voice he heard on the phone contained the exact same tone of alarm.

"They're going to keep multiplying!" Dale said. "The old woman was right. It's all part of the Soggon's grand plan to take over the town. You've got to get out of there. Now!"

"Dale, listen," Wilson said. "There's no such thing as a swamp creature that can turn people into scarecrows. It's a prank. An elaborate and complicated one, for sure. But a prank. I'll get to the bottom of it, okay?"

"No, Mr. Kendrick. Don't hang up! Don't go back out there! It's not safe!"

"Dale," Wilson said in as calm a voice as he could. "Listen. I'm sorry I woke you. I'm sorry to have bothered you. It's fine. It's all fine. Good night."

He placed the receiver back in the cradle and shook his head again. "Swamp skoggin' indeed," he muttered. "Or was it a soakun?" He let out a short laugh. Nothing shed the substantive light of reason on a situation more than listening to someone who had lost all voice of reason. Hearing Dale go on about the dangers of a nasty swamp monster washed all nonsense about the ghosts of his mother's mythology from his mind.

And he was even more determined to get to the bottom of how these pranksters were perpetuating this hoax. Particularly since they likely hadn't expected him to wake up and "catch" them in the act – thus their ability to remain undetected despite his ongoing investigation spoke highly of their skill at quick adaptation.

But they must have access to a convenient storage facility.

The Saunderson's barn just across the road seemed the most likely place.

Wilson put his jacket back on and headed out the front door to go have a look. The Saundersons had a teenage son. Perhaps he was involved in this with several of his friends.

As he moved through the front yard, he didn't bother trying to remain undetected. The pranksters obviously knew he was out and about and were maintaining the charade of continuing to plant the scarecrow army into their posts while remaining undetected. As he walked across the front lawn, Wilson counted another half dozen scarecrows. Among them were several children figures. Some of them weren't standing; two of them were leaning against trees, and one was sitting atop a boulder. He chuckled at one that seemed to be lying atop the roof of the shed at the end of the turn-around in his driveway.

As he crossed the highway, he thought he could hear the cacophony of knitting needles he'd heard earlier, and he stopped in the middle of the road to listen. But like before, the sound faded as quickly as it had come on and he continued along.

The fog was thicker on this side of the highway, being that much closer to the sea's edge, and it carried with it a heavier, more pervasive scent of the salty sea air. The rhythmic lapping of the waves on the nearby shoreline was also louder and offered him a sense of calm and normalcy.

Wilson didn't notice the Saunderson car in the driveway until he had traversed almost halfway up the drive and was just a few feet away from it. As he walked past the black Volkswagen Passat he noted the droplets of dew on it but still touched the hood to feel that the engine underneath it was cold. If they had gone away this past weekend on one of their regular family trips they had definitely arrived back a long time ago.

Wilson was walking past the Saunderson house on his way to the barn when he spotted a figure standing on the front porch. He stopped and raised his hand in greeting but then quickly lowered it when he realized it wasn't Eric Saunderson, but a scarecrow. He took a few steps forward.

"Well I'll be damned," Wilson whispered. This scarecrow looked just like his neighbour Eric Saunderson, complete with the red plaid hunting jacket he always wore on cool fall evenings, the horn-rimmed glasses and the distinct and particular hair patch on the crown of his head. The scarecrow had a small round circle of hair on the top middle of his head, separated from the rest of the receding hairline like some inlet island. It was a perfect match to the island of hair Saunderson boasted.

Wilson laughed, completely impressed with the detail.

But it didn't make sense to him that the pranksters would go to that much pain, particularly with this scarecrow being completely out of visual range from his own front step.

A chill ran up Wilson's spine.

There was something more amiss here than he'd been willing to admit.

A car turning the corner down the highway threw a fog blurred headlight beam across the front of the Saunderson house. In that quick flash of subdued light Wilson saw one of the Saunderson children sitting on the front step swing, or rather, the likeness of the young girl in scarecrow guise. And behind her, visible through the front window, was the likeness of Pamela Saunderson, in her blue pansy print house dress, still holding the television remote in her right hand.

For the second time that night, Wilson turned and ran back to his house.

As he ran, he held his right arm strategically over his mouth and nose, fearful of breathing in a toxic substance and tried to ignore the fact that at least two or three more scarecrows had appeared in previously vacant spots in his yard.

The phone was ringing when he got inside.

Out of breath, he stumbled to the phone.

"Hello?" Wilson huffed into the phone as he picked it up.

"Mr Kendrick?" It was Dale. "The phone kept ringing. I was scared you'd gone outside. Thank God you answered. Don't go outside. Don't go anywhere near the swamp. If you can get to your shed without being seen, here's what you need to do. You need to-"

"Dale!" Wilson interrupted, finally catching his breath. "Stop it! There is definitely something going on. I think it's some sort of airborne contagion. I've never seen anything like it, but I've formulated a quick theory. I haven't thought it through completely, but . . ." Wilson stopped talking, realizing he was rambling on in the same manner Dale had been.

In the run back to his house he determined that what he was seeing might have been caused by some airborne substance, possibly carried in from the sea on the fog. He suspected it was causing a reaction not unlike the side effects one might see with Tetrodotoxin. It made sense, given that this deadly neurotoxin was found in puffer fish and some species of marine toads and tree frogs and that the side effect was paralyses and the appearance of death. Wilson amused himself by noting it was a Canadian ethno botanist, Wade Davis, who had created a pharmacological case for zombies in his studies and research.

He deduced that the neurotoxin, which could be passed into the bloodstream through topical exposure, was somehow carried on the fog and causing the zombie-like appearance in the victims. The reason people might have seemed to appear out of nowhere on Wilson's front lawn could be due to confusion – another side effect of the poisoning – and mass panic.

All these thoughts and theories, still not completely resolved were swirling in Wilson's head when he'd answered the phone. He'd made a rash error by blurting it out, particularly to a young man without the scientific knowledge or background to understand it.

"Mr. Kendrick. Are you still there?"

Wilson took a deep breath. "Yes, Dale. I am. Now listen. There is something seriously wrong going on.

You need to stay inside, keep the windows closed. And don't go out."

"But, Mr. Kendrick." Dale pleaded. "You've got to stop the Swamp Soggon. Fire will do it. Swamp creatures crave moisture. They're afraid of fire.

"There are a few ten-gallon gas cans in your shed. You can use them to dose the scarecrows then light them on fire. Burn them. Surround your house with a wall of flames. Don't let any of them, or the Swamp Soggon in."

Wilson recoiled at the b-movie antics Dale suggested; never mind that he was holding fast to some supernatural hocus-pocus theory of a swamp creature. The entire scenario he'd been suggesting was farcical.

Rather than continue with an argument he knew neither of them would budge on, Wilson thought his best course of action was to hang up and alert the authorities. Given that there was some airborne contagion, they needed to shut down the highway, establish the greater Moser River region as a hot zone.

"Dale," Wilson said. "I'm hanging up now. Whatever you do, stay inside. Keep the windows and doors closed." Dale lived several kilometers down the highway in a neighboring community, and Wilson couldn't be sure how far the contagion might have spread. With that said, he pushed his finger down on the receiver disconnect button.

When he lifted his finger a moment later Dale was still there. The young man hadn't hung up and the line hadn't disconnected.

"Dale," Wilson said calmly. "Please hang up."

There was no response on the other end.

He placed the receiver down in the cradle.

Waited a moment.

Picked it up again.

Still, dead air. No dial tone.

Dale still hadn't hung up.

Then Wilson listened and couldn't even hear the young man breathing. Maybe the young man had dropped the phone. Perhaps after having fallen prey to the toxin, a panicked thought raced through the back of his head.

"Dale!" Wilson shouted. "Dale, are you there?"

But he was again greeted with nothing but silence.

"Damn!"

Wilson repeatedly jabbed at the release button but still didn't get any dial tone. He slammed the phone back in the cradle.

Standing over the telephone, Wilson hoped against hope that Dale was okay, that perhaps the young man was just too frightened to speak, and that's why there was no answer on the other end.

And he thought about what the young man had suggested. Dousing the scarecrows in flames. Creating a flame ring.

The young man had suggested it likely as a result of seeing too many black and white b-movies about the Creature from the Black Lagoon or something; but there was a point there. If this region of Highway 7 was falling prey to a local outbreak of some sort of contagion, he wondered if dousing the victims in gasoline then setting them aflame might help prevent further spread, at least until the proper authorities in charge of disease control could get out here.

He tried the phone once more.

It was still connected at Dale's end.

He plucked the keys to the padlock on the shed from the key hook in the front hall then rummaged in the utility drawer of the front hall table and found the Zippo lighter. He paused in front of the cherry oak framed mirror hanging on the wall above the table and looked at himself.

This could be it, he thought as he stared into the reflection of his own middle aged eyes, now very much droopy and tired looking. Going back out there would likely mean exposing himself to whatever toxin was currently floating around in the air on the fog. And it could mean certain death.

But, understanding what he did, there was a chance he could at least slow some of the spread of this down; lead authorities to discover what was happening.

He never thought of himself as a hero, even in the fantasies that played in the back of his mind. He was a software developer, an analytical business man with a keen thirst for knowledge and answers.

And though he had fallen in love once, he'd never had a single meaningful relationship, despite decades of trying; never had kids. Sure, he'd leave behind a small legacy with the software company and products he'd developed. But that would fade in time with the emerging of new and better technologies, multi-generational versions of his products.

He at least had this. He might be able to make a difference and slow down the outbreak. Wilson thought about the two main reasons he'd moved to Nova Scotia in the first place. Initially, it was in seeking the love of a woman; but he'd also had loftier pursuits. After retiring and having enough money to do whatever he wanted, move wherever he wished, Wilson decided to move to the region of his father's childhood and research the family history.

He'd learned all kinds of details about his family, about his heritage, and had compiled a huge file of facts that he'd posted on his blog. One of the proudest was the fact that he was a distant relative of Vince Coleman, the train dispatcher who'd stayed behind in the aftermath of a collision of two ships in Halifax harbor (one loaded with tons of dangerous explosives) to telegraph an urgent warning to an incoming passenger train. Coleman had died that morning along with 2000 others in the Halifax explosion of 1917; but not before saving the 700 lives of the people aboard the train he'd sent the warning to.

Wilson figured that the least he could do would be to carry on in that proud example of nobility.

He considered the fastest and best way to both get the word out as well as alert authorities would be via the internet. So, he ran into his study to boot up his computer. A quick single paragraph blog entry would explain what he was doing in case he didn't survive to tell the tale; and an auto blast of his message via an RSS feed sent out to all his contacts via two social networking platforms in which he boasted over 3000 "friends" – mostly other like-minded computer geeks and scientific minds – would likely reach the proper authorities in record time.

With that done, Wilson went to the kitchen, turned on all of the burners on the gas stove, then ripped a curtain off the kitchen window and laid it across the burners. They erupted into flame immediately, and he tossed the burning curtain back toward the window, watching it catch the other, still hanging curtain.

He fled out through the back door of the kitchen and raced to the shed at the side of his house.

By the time he got to the shed, the flames from inside the kitchen were so bright they lit up the entire back yard, and he was easily able to negotiate the key into the padlock. He flung open the shed door and in that same light was able to find the gas drums Dale had mentioned.

As he was hauling out the first steel drum, he caught sight of a scarecrow just a few yards to the right of the shed that he hadn't noticed before.

He dropped the drum and the lighter and stared at her.

"Ashley," he whispered, not able to take his eyes off the scarecrow, mesmerized by the way the flicker of the fire light danced in her short red hair.

He took a single step forward.

"No, please don't be Ashley. Please . . ."

He took another step forward, then another, until he was standing in front of her. He put his left hand up to feel the warmth of alabaster skin. His right hand stroked her silky red hair as he stared deep into those teal green eyes and thought back to the very first night he'd lost himself in them.

It had been a decade earlier. Wilson had flown in to Halifax to attend a tech conference. On an evening out with fellow delegates, he'd ended up at The Lower Deck, a bar down on the waterfront when a gorgeous young waitress caught his eye, or rather, his ear.

He overheard her discussion with an older couple at a neighboring table as she slid two bowls of clam chowder in front of them.

"I had a chat with the chef and wanted to assure you that this chowder, our house specialty, has absolutely no shell fish content in it."

"Thank you," the man said, dipping his head.

The waitress then pulled her notepad out and ripped off the first page. "And just to ensure you're aware of the contents, I had the chef list every single ingredient he used." She handed them the paper with a huge grin, winked and gently touched the arm of the old gentleman. "Now you just keep this paper confidential. We don't want any of our competitors finding out our special secret ingredients."

Laughing, the couple thanked her and she moved over to Wilson's table and introduced herself as Ashley.

The young woman was pleasant, sweet, courteous and charming and Wilson had never seen such a lovely smile.

Regardless of the entertaining musical show and great conversation with fellow delegates Wilson found that he could not keep his eyes off of the pretty red-head. It wasn't out of any sort of drunken lust -- he simply derived pleasure from gazing at her.

She'd noticed his stare early into the evening and often interpreted it as a sign that he needed another drink. Delighted to have an excuse to chat and flirt with her, Wilson continued to order rounds of drinks for the group at his table. Each time she came to the table, they exchanged short quick pleasantries and he was as enthralled with the sound of her voice as much as he had been with her cute close-mouthed smile. Through the course of the evening, she'd learned his first name and they'd fallen into a comfortable pattern of humorous exchanges.

When the bar closed and the other delegates had piled into cabs to head home, Wilson didn't want the wonderful evening to end. He was still high with the pleasures of flirting with Ashley and admiring her pixie-like beauty all evening. He'd never been particularly smooth or popular with women, so he was surprised at how calm and natural joking around with her had been. So, trying to stretch out the evening, he took a stroll on the docks to bask in the smell of the sea air, the sounds of the ships creaking in the movement of the waves, the lights of Dartmouth across the water. His hotel was at the south end of the docks, so he'd ventured north on a short stroll, exploring a bit before turning around and heading back.

Just a few yards past where The Lower Deck was, he spotted Ashley walking along the deck ahead of him. She turned her head slightly when she heard the echo of his footsteps on the boardwalk and smiled when she recognized him.

"Hi, Wilson. I didn't figure you for a stalker," she said, still smiling.

He laughed and his face turned red. "It's just so incredibly beautiful out here," he said, one arm waving toward the water. Then he turned back toward her, the beer speaking the next words. "So incredibly beautiful. Like you."

Wilson paused, realizing what he'd just done. His jaw dropped open. He'd never been so forward with a woman before, imagined what he'd just said sounded like a goofy pick-up line. He had no idea how she'd react.

Ashley smiled, then laughed. "Thanks. But you're drunk. All girls look pretty to you right now." She offered out her elbow to him. "C'mon. Take my arm. I'll make sure you make it back safely to your hotel."

He tentatively hooked his elbow around hers.

"But just to warn you," she grinned as they started walking together. "You make any funny moves and I'm tossing you right into the drink. I have a black belt in karate and Jujitsu."

"Really?"

"No, I'm just pulling your leg. But for a scrawny little chick I'm tough, and I'll lift you over my head and throw you into the water as sure as I'm standing here."

Wilson laughed. "I don't doubt for a second you're capable of it. But I doubt you'd hurt a flea."

"Not true," she grinned wryly. "I've killed plenty of fleas in my time. Mosquitoes, black flies and spiders too."

He laughed again. "You're a walking exterminator."

It was a forty-five-minute walk to the end of the boardwalk where Wilson's hotel was. Wilson soaked in the details about Ashley's life and was as impressed with her as he was with the picturesque scenery.

They couldn't have been more opposite in their backgrounds and views on life, but Wilson admired everything about her. A farm girl from a small town a few hours outside of Halifax, she'd graduated from the local University and had been working as a waitress in the evenings since her second year in University to pay for school. And since graduating, she also had a day job working afternoons at a nearby restaurant. She had at least another year of working the two jobs before she'd be done paying her student loans. Once that was done, she would take her B.A. back to the dairy farm near Moser

River which her father still ran, and apprentice herself to take over the business.

Wilson couldn't fathom why someone would return to the hard and rugged routine of farm life after earning themselves a post-secondary education that could land them a better job.

But this just led to the mystique of Ashley, and what became his decade long infatuation with her.

When they were within sight of the end of the boardwalk, they stood near a large docked fishing vessel and talked for another forty minutes. The conversation hadn't even come close to running dry, but a drizzle of rain brought it to a quick end.

"It has been great chatting with you," Ashley said, her green eyes beaming. She kissed him briefly on the cheek before turning and walking away. "You're a sweet man. Goodnight, Wilson. Have a safe flight back home."

"Goodbye Ashley," Wilson simply grinned and waved goodbye as she headed toward Morris street to her apartment.

He stood there and watched her retreat, not taking his eyes off of her until she completely disappeared from view, thinking he'd never again see this magnificent woman whom he felt so naturally comfortable with. He remained motionless for another few minutes, still basking in her warmth as he stood alone on the dock, barely noticing the cold rain plastering his clothes to his skin.

For years after that meeting, Wilson wondered if the rain had been the perfect cue to invite her to his hotel room.

Of course, Wilson had never been a smooth operator and that single hour of conversation with her was the closest he'd ever come to having a relationship with a woman. Pathetic, he knew. But his heart never stopped burning for Ashley, and she had been a good part of the reason he'd decided to retire in Halifax. Sure, there'd been the desire to research his family background, but there'd also been Ashley -- and Wilson often didn't make a decision unless there were two solid deciding factors to prompt him.

When he'd returned a decade after meeting her – six months ago now – and looked her up, he was overwhelmingly disappointed to find she'd gotten married five years earlier and already had a three year old son. He didn't bother contacting her, figuring she wouldn't remember him anyway, but had continued to admire her from afar, at least somewhat content to know she was happy and prosperous.

Until now.

The virus had gotten to her.

Wilson stood before the woman he'd loved and yearned for and let his tears flow.

"I loved you from the moment we first met, Ashley," Wilson said, his words wet and heavy. "And I never stopped loving you all these years."

Then he did something he'd never dared do before.

He leaned forward and placed a single gentle kiss on Ashley's lips.

Like the others, her latex-like flesh was warm.

Then he took a step back to admire her again. Even in this grotesque and creepy scarecrow form, she was as beautiful and glowing as he first remembered her. He continued to stand and admire her, never tiring of the pleasure of gazing into her eyes.

As he stared into those glassy green orbs, he saw a tear well up in the corner of her eye socket and run down her face. Imagining it was just moisture from the fog gathering there, he dismissed it, until a second tear strolled down after it a moment later.

"Ashley?" Wilson said, his words barely a whisper.

He reached forth, brought a single finger up to the tear rolling down her cheek and caught it on his finger tip. The tear was warm.

"Ashley?" he repeated. "Oh dear, sweet Ashley. Are you still alive in there?"

The strange incessant clicking noise he'd heard earlier sounded again and something sharp jabbed into Wilson's right ankle.

He yelled and stumbled backward as he kicked at the source of the pain. A black crow scampered off across the grass. Despite the fog, his eyes were able to track it as it ran, flapping its wings to gain forward momentum, all the way to the edge of the forest adjacent to his property.

That was when he noticed something strange about the trees – and since he hadn't actually looked at them before he'd not picked up on it already. But the trees seemed alive with small subtle movement, not unlike the rustling of leaves in the trees. Only, there wasn't any wind and the leaves were dark, shadowy things. As he looked at the trees, Wilson could now see they were filled to capacity with crows. Every single tree. Thousands of black birds sat in the branches.

A subtle shift in the wind brought the clicking noise to him, the sound of thousands of old ladies madly knitting coming from those very same trees.

An intense burning cold sensation, like the feeling of anesthetic running through his veins, started at his ankle and shot up his leg. He turned back to look at Ashley, and her beautiful green eyes were the last thing he saw before he blacked out.

Wilson didn't so much open his eyes as much as his consciousness rose to slowly reveal the world in front of him like some dark black stage curtain falling away.

He was standing in his back yard, at about the spot he'd been in when he took a step back from Ashley. He couldn't turn his head, his neck was stiff and tight, like he'd slept with his head at a funny angle, but he could see Ashley.

And beyond her, the other scarecrows, hundreds of them. Faintly, softly in the background, he could still hear that maddening chorus of quiet clicking.

That's when he realized it hadn't been a dream. The whole evening had been real.

He looked back and forth as he tried to move his arms, take a step forward.

His limbs were heavy and useless. He couldn't move them at all.

The virus, the disease, whatever it was, it was being spread by those crows. Perhaps generated by the crows. Wilson tried to listen to them, watch the trees for further signs of their movement.

"I didn't know."

The softly spoken words came clearly from his right, and though he hadn't heard it in ten years Wilson had never forgotten the sweet melodic tone of Ashley's voice.

"Didn't know what?" Wilson spoke without moving his lips, but his voice was clear and normal.

"How you felt about me."

"You . . . remember me?"

"Of course I do, Wilson. How couldn't I? You were a sweet guy, and I could tell you were interested in me as a person and not just trying to lure me into the nearest bed. Before you, I'd never met a man who didn't just want into my pants. How could I forget something like that?"

Wilson didn't answer, he just strained to look at Ashley from the corner of his eye.

"But you never called. I thought about you for a long time. I always wondered where you were or what you'd been up to. Of course, after time, I realized I didn't really know you – that you were just some fantasy man who'd walked into my life one evening and then walked out just as quickly.

"But thanks to you, showing me that there were sweet guys out there, it changed the way I looked at men. And I found someone sweet and genuine. My husband Robert is a great guy, Wilson. I was first attracted to him because he reminded me of you."

Wilson's vision blurred as tears welled up in his eyes. He thought of all of those lonely years of wondering about Ashley, how he'd sat around thinking of excuses to call her or look her up on the internet and get in contact with her. But he never worked up the courage to do anything.

It was only after he retired that he finally worked up the nerve to go seek her. But even then, he had the plan of researching his family history as a backup; thinking himself a fool for pursuing Ashley from the other side of the continent.

But by then it had been too late.

And now? Now, here they were, stuck in scarecrow form, partially facing one another and apparently unable to do anything but talk. Wilson felt a pang of bittersweet happiness.

"Ashley," he whispered, his voice still choked with tears. "I never stopped loving you. Never stopped longing to hear your sweet voice again, just be near you again. Talk to me. There's time now. More than enough time. So talk to me. Tell me something, anything. Please just talk to me, Ashley."

The muffled sound of footsteps on the damp leaf encrusted grass approached from behind him. But there was another noise, although Wilson couldn't quite figure out what it was.

"Someone's coming," Ashley said, hopefully. "Mister, Mister. Over here, please help us. Please."

Wilson looked and saw a single man walking in the grass, carefully avoiding coming too close to any of the scarecrow people he passed. Wilson figured out what the secondary sound was a moment later. It was the combined chorus of all the other scarecrow people calling to him for help in vain. He simply couldn't hear them, as if their voices were of a pitch too high for the naked human ear to detect.

As the man got closer, Wilson recognized him. Tall, obviously broad-shouldered even in his thick orange fall hunting jacket; a young, distinctly handsome man with short curly blonde hair and big brown wide eyes. It was Dale.

"Dale!" Wilson called out. "Over here. It's me. It's Wilson."

Even as he spoke the words, even as his cries to be heard merged with the pathetic chorus of pleas for help from the others, Wilson knew there was no point. But he couldn't stop himself from pleading, from begging.

His pleas turned to panicked yelling as he saw Dale walk over to the steel gas drum Wilson had dropped, take a quick look around, then pick up the drum and pull a lighter out of his pocket.

Despite the intensity of his own shrill screams, Wilson could still hear each of Dale's booted steps clearly as he marched toward him and Ashley and unscrewed the cap to the gas can.

As the gasoline splashed into his eyes, blinding him, the last thing Wilson heard before that final whomph of the flames igniting was Ashley's screams.

And the maddening clicking sound of the crows in the nearby trees.

Behind the Screams

I STILL RECEIVE emails and comments from readers who share that they quite enjoy the "behind the story" notes I add to the end of many of my short stories and collections of short fiction.

And so, I present here, a few insights and some background information either on the inspiration or source for each of the stories you have just read.

If you're not a person who enjoys watching the special features on a DVD or the movie along with commentary from the actors or director, then I suggest you simply stop reading now. Thanks for picking up this collection and reading a few of my stories. I hope you enjoyed them enough to want to read more of my fiction.

If, however, you do enjoy that "behind the curtains" peek into my fiction, then we still have a little bit of time left in our little post-midnight stroll. Just ignore those dancing shadows trailing along beside us, and let me bring your attention to some further background and insights into the tales you just read.

About "The Shadow Men"

Originally published in print in **Northern Haunts: 100 Terrifying New England Tales**, *edited by Tim Deal, (Shroud Publishing, 2008), and in eBook format in* **Bumps in the Night: Creepy Campfire Tales** *(2012).*

THE SHADOW MEN was written as a result of digging back into the concept of "The Bush People" from a story ("Erratic Cycles") which was published in **Parsec** magazine in the Winter of 1998.

For that original story, I had drafted a short back-story about some tale that the main character's father had shared with him around a campfire when he was young. Memories of that story helped enhance his fears of being in the woods after dark. But, in the way that minor "interesting touch" elements from a story can sometimes linger, the concept of "The Bush People" which evolved into "The Shadow Men" (because, honestly, it just sounded creepier), stayed with me.

When I was reading the guidelines for Tim Deal's anthology in which he wanted extremely short stories set in the New England wilderness, I reflected back to the tale that might have been shared around a campfire. And so I drew out the tale, looking to enhance the eerie feel to it.

But I didn't want to just draw out the tale. I wanted to write it in a style where, anyone who picked up the story, could read it aloud, perhaps even around a campfire, and share the tale as if it were something that had happened to them.

I felt that little extra touch added something unique and of its own.

I don't often write stories in which the narrator addresses the reader, but this is one of those that I think works quite nicely. And it's a story that I'll often use when doing public readings. Because it's extremely short, so the listeners aren't really going to drop off; they never really have a chance.

Admittedly, I haven't yet shared this tale around a campfire; but I hope to, one, day, be able to do that, drawing the story out just a little bit longer, and calling upon more elements into the story from the nearby sounds and sights from wherever we're camping.

Should you ever have the chance to do the same around a campfire, do feel free to liberate this tale into your own crafty tale. I'd love to hear from you if you tired it, at how it worked for your audience.

About "Follow the Shadow"

ONE EVENING WHILE walking alone down the street, I was watching how my shadow continued to change as I was moving.

When I was immediately under a streetlight, it was a simple mass of dark blob under my feet.

And as I walked away, leaving the streetlight behind me, my shadow began to slowly stretch out in front of me, eventually evolving from a squished-like mass and into a short and stubby, then longer man.

But, just before the shadow could reach out and become too much taller than me, it's thickness began to fade. The streetlight I had left behind was now farther away, casting less power towards creating my shadow. But the streetlight that I was now getting closer to was beginning to create a long, tall shadow cast behind me.

As the shadow before me faded into virtual non-existence, the one behind me became stronger, tighter, and moved back slowly, to eventually be that similar mass of dark blob under my feet.

Normally, when I'm walking by myself after dark I'm a little apprehensive. I mean, I still believe in the monster under the bed. I am always leery of dark and shadowy places, because, after all, that's usually where I'm drawing from the well on inspiration for my writing. So, when I'm walking at night my mind is constantly conjugating all the possible nasty things waiting just around the next corner or lurking, just out of sight, in the dark shadows.

However, that night, I amused myself by watching the cyclical movement of my shadow, or, more accurately, shadows, as I moved from block to block, under streetlight after streetlight. The shadows that pulsed behind, under and in front of me were like waves coming on to a beach, an eternal pattern.

But, I also wondered if I were watching some sort of endless lifecycle of a shadow. And I marveled at how the shadows life was so dependent on the proximity to a source of light.

So I tucked those thoughts away.

Some time later, while walking by myself during the day, and paying attention to my shadow, which was a lot more consistent under the tutelage of the afternoon sun, I reflected at how children were often fascinated with their own shadows (not unlike me – but I'll readily admit that my mind hasn't ever really left childhood, or at least, the ceaseless curiosity that children possess). You often see kids trying to outrun their shadow, trying to jump to get away from it touching them. Making rash and sudden movements in an attempt to thwart the shadow's constant and 100% accurate mocking of their own movements. Always, of course, to no avail. Because there's no escaping that shadow version of yourself.

Children will sometimes laugh and run after each other's shadow, stomping on their friends' shadow and laughing; the friend, laughing and shrieking for them to stop, as if stepping on their shadow is stepping on their toes. And, in a more systematic fashion, there's always "Shadow Tag" which plays just like the classic game of "It" except, instead of tagging the person, you have to tag their shadow, usually by stepping on it.

But it's always about the human controlling where the shadow goes.

It's never about the shadow controlling where the human goes.

So, what if that could happen?

Reflecting on all these things, I came up with the first line. But, as I was writing the story, I wondered if the shadow was actually controlling the narrator, or if he were merely suffering a psychotic episode.

And that's where the story came from.

I don't think that I'm actually done toying with this concept in stories. I know that there are at least two other "takes" on the shadows controlling the person that I will likely pen.

Because, much like that shadow of mine that always comes out, always teases me when I'm walking alone at night, the story will begin inside me, just a dark blob of a mass, but then, as I move along, it will eventually grow, take form and establish itself as something unique and of its own; but of course, a reflection of part of me.

About "A Murder of Scarecrows"

SOMETIMES A STORY is born out of multiple elements swirling around, collected and gathered and lovingly cared for over time. But other times a story is created in a single inspired burst of inspiration that keeps me up all night.

"A Murder of Scarecrows" is that type of story.

But first, let me break this down to give a little bit of a background in pieces, to explain this story's origin.

The Scarecrows of Necum Teuch

There's a small village in Nova Scotia about 50 kilometers (30 miles) from Sheet Harbour and a two hour drive East of Halifax called Necum Teuch. It lies between the communities of Moser River and Ecum Secum. There isn't much to this tiny community, however it has captured the eyes and imaginations of those who drive past slow enough to behold a most unusual sight.

Scattered about the yard, garden and adjacent swamp of an otherwise unassuming white house at the edge of a highway is a small army of scarecrows.

And not just regular scarecrows, but ones that are meant to look a bit more human than most.

They were originally the creation of an Angella Geddes, who, in 1998, created and named them all (offering them names such as Aunt Mary, Captain Smith and Miss Marie Marlene). They were part of a legend she created and shared that featured an "ugly" and selfish creature called the "Swamp Soggon" who, one day, grew angry and turned virtually everybody in the town of Necum Teuch into scarecrows.

The legend and scarecrows were immortalized in a book published by Nimbus in 1996 entitled "The Scarecrows of Necum Teuch." The book explained the legend, included a scarecrow game, instructions on how to make your own scarecrow as well as a recipe for Aunt Mary's "Unspeakable" soup.

Angella Geddes continued to grow her army of scarecrows until she died suddenly in 2006. Apparently, friends, family and locals kept up the tradition and have done their best to preserve the unique characters who pepper the landscape.

I recently discovered <u>an online article, written in 2013, by Peter Duchemin</u>, that tells a little bit about his own experience meeting Angella and having a tour of her wondrous creations. It's a fun story and worth a read if you're curious for more information.

The Origin of "A Murder of Scarecrows"

Between 2006 and 2011 I worked for the McMaster University Bookstore. One of the great pleasures of this job was getting to meet with campus store colleagues from across the country at events such as the twice-yearly Campus Store Canada gatherings. In November of 2007, the CSC group met for a week in Halifax.

During a couple of free nights, I booked myself in to a few book signings, and on the Saturday night, I drove my rental car through the nasty hurricane Noel which was hitting the East Coast of Canada, to the Chapters at Bayers Lake. It was a relatively quiet night, although I was impressed with the conviction of locals. I was quite terrified with the hurricane so close, but they seemed to be going about their business nonplussed about the whole matter.

My table was adjacent to the connected Starbucks and I ended up chatting with a barista named Ashley who enjoyed spooky tales. She picked up a copy of my short story collection *One Hand Screaming*, and we shared a few of our favorite recent reads with one another. A student at one of the local colleges, she was an avid reader and book lover. Her enthusiasm and love for books shone very clearly in her eyes.

Later in the evening, Ashley came back to the table to tell me about a place not all that far away that she thought I might be interested in. It was Necum Teuch. And it concerned the scarecrows that Angella Geddes had populated the town with. But there was something about the way Ashley told me the story that made it seem as if the scarecrows were multiplying entirely on their own.

I couldn't stop thinking about the scarecrows and this small town.

And on the drive back to my hotel, a drive in which I recall swerving on the highway to avoid a huge pile of debris that must have blown from the back of a truck in the hurricane-force winds, all I kept thinking about was how much I wanted to write about this place. For a few moments I was worried I might not make it home to write the story. (Yes, that's just how passionate I can get when a story that needs to be written takes hold).

I got back to my hotel close to midnight and immediately logged on to the Internet and looked for details about Necum Teuch and the scarecrows. I found a few articles about them as well as some eerie pictures. I jotted down some notes and descriptions of a few of the scarecrows, and then begin to write the story.

As I wrote, the howling winds of hurricane Noel hammered against the hotel. I was on the ninth floor and every once in a while I paused to look out the window at the trees being forced over in the strong winds.

I wrote about 4000 or so words before I noticed that several hours had passed. I rather love losing myself in a story so much that I lose complete track of time. I made a few notes about where I wanted the story to go and then crawled into bed at about 3:30 AM.

The hurricane ended up taking out the power in the hotel – but that only added to the wonderful sense of fear coursing through me. Ashley had also emailed me a few further details that I had asked for, as well as letting me know that her father was planning a trip that would take him through Necum Tuech within the next week, with an offer to take some pictures and send them to me.

The following night, after a fun evening out with my colleagues at a local pub, I finished the first draft of the story. It came in at about 10,000 words.

I put the story aside for about a week and then came back to it. As a thank-you to Ashley and her father Dale for the background details and help provided, I decided to change my character names to honor them. At that time I also spent some time trying to establish Dale's character a little bit more. By the time I was finished, the second draft came in at 12,000 words. I then focused on whittling the story down and cutting out some of the extra details that didn't either move the story forward or assist with illuminating the characters.

After a few more drafts, I ended up with a version of "The Murder of Scarecrows" that I was happy with.

I still haven't been to Necum Tuech to see the scarecrows for myself. I returned to Halifax in the Fall of 2018 to participate as a writer in Halifax *Word on the Street*. I'd been hoping to have had time to rent a car and drive out there to see if any of the scarecrows are still there. But I stayed within the city, on foot, and ended up investigating the spirit of so many incredible craft beer breweries the city had to offer.

You might say I substituted straw for barley and hops.

Conclusion: One Last Shadowy Cry

THANKS FOR TAKING a walk with me along the dark and shadowy streets. I hope that you enjoyed the stories (and the stories behind the stories) as much as I enjoyed writing them.

I began my writing journey with short stories, and they will always hold a special place in my heart. Short stories, particularly in the horror genre, allow an author to be experimental, and, of course, since there's not as much time and energy invested in a character by the reader, can easily take a darker turn for the ending.

The dark shadows from which I draw so much of my inspiration comes not only from my fear of the dark, but from the shadow play I have done my entire life. As a child, I marveled at the way my own shadow would mock every single move I made. But would also play with how, using different angles of light and different body parts, I could morph shadows into being something unique and interesting and looking not of this world.

When I was in university, I worked backstage as a stagehand and assistant stage manager and as a lighting designer, and I realized how marvelously one could use light in different ways to enhance a story. For one play where I was the lighting designer, *Lolita*, I used special effects in lighting to enhance two particular scenes.

One, in which the young girl strips naked in front of Humbert Humbert, the actress was actually naked, but the back-lighting used in that scene not only enhanced the dramatic effect of her revealing herself to him, but prevented the audience from seeing everything. She was perfectly back-lit so that her naked body's form could be seen, but details remained hidden from the audience. A perfect effect that also preserved some of the more private elements of the actress' body.

The other, where Lolita's mother is standing at the top of the stairs and pointing a gun at Humbert Humbert, she takes a spill down the stairs and dies. Such a scene, on stage, would be too difficult to choreograph without the actress harming herself, so the stairway was imagined as being just offstage. Using lighting, we created a marvelous effect where Humbert Humbert stands in horror as this giant looming shadow of the woman holding the gun is cast from backstage. Her shadow is much larger than him, giving it the proper menacing effect. Then, for her fall, it was a matter of playing with the shadow to denote her tumble, along with perfectly timed sound effects, with the actress finally rolling, as if dead, onto the stage at the end of the tumble.

Shadows can be powerful. In theatre, in story and in real life.

Perhaps now, after reading this collection of short tales, you might pay just a little more attention to the shadows that you cast, or that you notice creeping toward you from the corner of your peripheral vision.

If you enjoyed this collection, I would greatly appreciate if you took the time to leave a review. It might seem like a small thing, but the one or two minutes it takes goes an incredibly long way towards helping a writer find new readers. And if you're so inclined to send me a note to let me know what you thought, that would be wonderful. My email is mark@markleslie.ca. (You can also sign up for my newsletter at www.markleslie.ca to stay informed of my new releases and get a full-sized eBook for free)

On the other hand, if you weren't satisfied with what you read, I'm happy to get an email from you just the same. Your experience and thoughts are just as important. I'm constantly looking to grow as a writer, and learning why a story didn't work for a reader can be an important part of that process.

In either case, thanks for accompanying me on this walk among the shadows and listening to some of those nocturnal screams with me. Perhaps, one day, we shall encounter each other either between the digital pages of another book, or maybe in person at some bookish event. If that happens, do say hello. Don't just be a shadow that passes by undiscovered.

- Mark Leslie
Sept 2020

About the Author

Mark Leslie is a writer, editor, and bookseller who was born and grew up in Sudbury, Ontario, spent many years in Ottawa, Ontario and currently lives in Southern Ontario. Claiming that he has always been frightened of the monster under his bed, Mark loves crafting eerie and creepy tales that follow the "what if" questions that occur to him every time he takes a peek into the shadows. And he spends a lot of times looking at the shadows and listening for the screams. You can learn more about Mark and sign up for his author newsletter at **www.markleslie.ca**.

Selected Other Books by Mark Leslie

Novels
A Canadian Werewolf in New York
Evasion
I, Death

Short Story Collections
One Hand Screaming
Active Reader
Nobody's Hero

Anthologies (as Editor)

Campus Chills
Tesseracts Sixteen: Parnassus Unbound
Fiction River: Editor's Choice
Fiction River: Feel the Fear
Fiction River: Feel the Love
Fiction River: Superstitious

Non-Fiction / Paranormal / Ghost Stories

Haunted Hamilton
Spooky Sudbury
Tomes of Terror
Creepy Capital
Haunted Hospitals
Macabre Montreal

The NOCTURNAL SCREAMS Series

 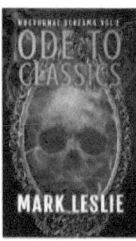